Underground Train

Cleveland Park

Nana

Woodley Park-Zoo

Red Line

Dupont Circle

Farragut North

Metro Center

Gallery Place

Archives

Green Line

L'Enfant Plaza

Waterfront Station

My underground train path to Nana

Underground Train

Mary Quattlebaum

illustrated by Cat Bowman Smith

A Doubleday Book for Young Readers

A Doubleday Book for Young Readers
Published by
Bantam Doubleday Dell Publishing Group, Inc.
1540 Broadway
New York, New York 10036
Doubleday and the portrayal of an anchor with a dolphin are trademarks of
Bantam Doubleday Dell Publishing Group, Inc.

Library of Congress Cataloging-in-Publication Data

Quattlebaum, Mary.
    Underground train / by Mary Quattlebaum ; illustrated by Cat Bowman Smith.
        p.   cm.
    Summary: A ride on the subway with Mama provides many vivid and exciting
sights and sounds.
    ISBN 0-385-32204-6
    [1. Subways–Fiction.   2. City and town life–Fiction.]
    I. Smith, Cat Bowman, ill.   II. Title.
    PZ7.Q19Un   1997
    [E]–dc20   96-30507
                                                                                CIP
                                                                                AC

The text of this book is set in 28-point Lemonade.
Book design by Trish Parcell Watts
Manufactured in the United States of America
November 1997
10 9 8 7 6 5 4 3 2 1

In memory of Nana
and the thrill of trips to see her
—M.Q.

For little Gabriel,
who already knows
about underground trains
—C.B.S.

The moving stairs roll us down, down, down to the underground train,

which rushes past like fast water on miles of track.

Rrrruuuummm. Whoooosshh.

I grip my fare and Mama grips my hand as the train doors slip aside like silver drapes. We step inside; the doors slide shut.

Rrrruuuummm. Whoooosshh.

The train starts slow and picks up speed.
I choose an orange seat
and watch the tunnel blurring by
like a long, black night.

Rrrruuuummm. Whoooosshh.

The train inside is filled with light.
Folks clutch their bags and smile
or read the news or yawn or talk.
The driver calls the stop:

Waterfront. Some people leave
and others take their seats;
then the bell sounds once, and the bright train starts
its rush into the dark.

Above the train, above my head, the busy city spreads: a map

of tangled streets and shops, cars, buildings, flags, clocks.

Above the train, above my head, a green light turns to red.

The traffic halts; the people cross.

Some sparrows hop in lots
beside the zoo, where lions snooze

and monkeys snack on fruit,
where zebras shake their manes and neigh
high, high above the train,

which rolls below the skipping feet

of two girls leaping neat and fleet

through double ropes that smack the sidewalk; whackity-whack!

Some kids race by on Rollerblades
and napping babies wake
with coos or cries as parents stroll

the place where Nana holds
a bag of bread and waits for me
to help her feed the geese and ducks.

Oh, high, high, high above,
the busy city moves
and shoves, skips, snacks, waits–

while down below, the train goes fast, fast, fast through miles

of dark until the driver halts and calls out *Cleveland Park.*

My stop.

The bright doors part. We walk
beside the quiet train. I pay
my fare. I step and sway

onto the stairs, which roll us up,
roll me and Mama up,
up, up until the sunshine streams
across the tangled streets,

the racing kids, the waiting geese;

and Nana waves at me.

Before I leave, I hear the sound
of something underground.

Rrrruuuummm. Whoooosshh.

Below the earth, below my feet,
the train is gaining speed
and rushing to the nearest stop
where folks step on and off.

Rrrruuuummm. Whoooosshh.

And then it starts again, far down,
down, down in the underground.
Below the earth, below my shoes,

Rrrruuuummm. Whoooosshh.

the lighted train continues.